PAPERBACK **PLUS**

Table of Contents

The Rat and the Tiger 4
a story by Keiko Kasza

Big and Little Friends 33
a photo essay about how animals help each other

Furry and Fierce Tigers! 36
an article from National Geographic World *magazine*

Meet Keiko Kasza

Keiko Kasza grew up in Japan. She lived with her two brothers and her parents and grandparents. Now she lives in the United States with her husband and two sons.

When Keiko Kasza wrote *The Rat and the Tiger*, she had to remember what it was like to be little.

The Rat and the Tiger

Keiko Kasza

HOUGHTON MIFFLIN COMPANY

BOSTON

ATLANTA   DALLAS   GENEVA, ILLINOIS   PALO ALTO   PRINCETON

Acknowledgments

For each of the selections listed below, grateful acknowledgment is made for permission to excerpt and/or reprint original or copyrighted materials, as follows:

Selections

"Furry and Fierce Tigers!" from *National Geographic World* magazine, August 1991. Copyright © 1991 by *National Geographic World. World* is the official magazine for Junior Members of the National Geographic Society. Reprinted by permission.

The Rat and the Tiger, by Keiko Kasza. Copyright © 1993 by Keiko Kasza. Reprinted by permission of G.P. Putnam's Sons, a division of the Putnam and Grosset Group.

Photography

33 Frans Lanting/Minden Pictures (background). **34** Stuart Westmoreland/Tony Stone Images (t); David Thompson, Oxford Scientific Films/Animals Animals (b). **35** David Fritts/Tony Stone Images (t); Tim Davis/Tony Stone Images (b). **36–37** Gerard Lace/Peter Arnold, Inc. **38** A & M Shah/Animals Animals.

To my parents

4

I'm a rat, just a tiny little rat.
Tiger is a big tough fellow.
We are best friends.

   We used to have a little problem, though. . . .

Whenever we played cowboys,
Tiger was always the good guy,
and I was the bad guy.

6

Tiger said, "The good guy always wins in the end."
What could I say? I'm just a tiny little rat.

7

Whenever Tiger and I shared a doughnut, Tiger always cut it so that his piece was bigger than mine.

8

Tiger said, "It's nice to share, isn't it?"
What could I say? I'm just a tiny little rat.

Whenever Tiger saw a flower he liked,
he just pointed and expected me
to get it for him.

Tiger said, "Isn't nature beautiful?"
What could I say? I'm just a tiny little rat.

One day I built a castle, the biggest one
I had ever made.

"Look, Tiger!" I shouted proudly.

Tiger said, "Nice job, Rat."

14

Then he jumped into the air and kicked my castle to pieces!

15

16

"That's it, Tiger!" I screamed.
"You're not my friend anymore.
I may be a tiny little rat
but you're a big mean bully!
Good-bye!"

I was mad. And I was sad.
But most of all, I was scared.
I had never yelled at Tiger like that before.

When Tiger found me, my heart almost stopped. I thought he might kick me just like he had kicked my castle.

"Go away, Tiger!" I shouted.

"I'm not afraid of you. Leave me alone!"

21

But Tiger didn't come to kick me.
He had fixed my castle, and he
wanted me to see it. So I did.
  But I told him, "I'm still not
your friend."

Then Tiger asked me if I wanted to play the good cowboy for a change. So I did.

But I told him, "I'm still not your friend."

Next, Tiger asked me if I wanted to cut our doughnut for once.
So I did.

But I told him, "I'm still not your friend."

Finally, Tiger asked me if I wanted a flower. So I pointed to one, and Tiger bravely went to pick it for me.

"Maybe," I told him, "just maybe I'll be your friend again."
Tiger smiled.

Ever since that day, we have gotten along just fine.
We take turns at everything. And we split
our doughnuts right down the middle.

We do have a little problem, though. . . .

A new kid on the block!

Big and Little Friends

Big: African Buffalo

Little: Cattle Egret

These birds peck off ticks, flies, and other pests that bite.

33

Big: Sea Anemone
Little: Clownfish

The clownfish is not hurt by the stingers on the anemone — but other fish get stung. When a clownfish is in danger, it stays close to the anemone to keep safe.

Big: Blue Butterfly Caterpillar
Little: Red Ant

This ant is taking care of a caterpillar. The ant gives food to the caterpillar, and the caterpillar makes sugary little drops that ants like to eat.

Big: Marine Iguana
Little: Red Rock Crab

There are ticks on these lizards. The lizards let red rock crabs crawl all over them and eat the insects.

Big: Rhinoceros
Little: Red-billed Oxpeckers

This oxpecker is cleaning insects off the rhinoceros. It also can see much better than the rhinoceros. When danger is near, the bird gives a warning.

Furry and Fierce
Tigers!

When these tiger cubs grow up, they'll be B-I-G. Tigers are the largest cats in the animal kingdom.

Tigers start out tiny. At birth, these cubs were smaller than house cats.

Now they are nearly two months old, and their eyes have opened.

In about four more months, the cubs will travel with their mother and learn to hunt.

On the alert, a six-month-old cub travels with its mother. By watching her, the cub will learn how to bring down prey.